The Evil Eye

Written and illustrated by
Oisín McGann

For David, who has a good eye.

First published in 2009 in Great Britain by
Barrington Stoke Ltd
18 Walker St, Edinburgh, EH3 7LP

www.barringtonstoke.co.uk

ISBN: 978-1-84299-631-7

Printed in Great Britain by Bell & Bain Ltd

Contents

Chapter 1
Into the Whirl-pool

High up in the stone tower, a woman screamed. Her begging and her sobs rang through the darkness. For a moment it was silent. Then came the sound of heavy feet making their way down from the top of the tower to the door below.

A huge shape loomed at the door of the tower. It was Balor, king of the Formorians. He was a monster, taller than any man and stronger than any warrior. His grey skin was pulled tight over massive muscles. A spiky fin ran from the top of his head to the middle of his back. There was webbing between his fingers and toes. He had the gills of a fish on his neck. But the most horrible thing about him was his face.

Balor was a terrible warrior, but his greatest weapon was not his sword, nor his spear or his club. His left eye was small and wrinkled, almost blind. He could not see much with this eye. But it opened and shut like a normal eye. His right eye was enormous – a great lump in the side of his head. The lids of this eye were closed. When this eye opened, people died.

In his arms Balor had a basket. And from the basket came the shrieks of three babies. They cried out for their mother.

Balor walked away from the tower. He walked across Tory Island to his castle. His castle was Tor Mor, a fortress where he lived with his people – the Fomorians – high up on a cliff. Balor strode to the edge of the cliff and looked down at the sea. Far below him, the sea crashed against the rocks. Further out, in the dark waters, a huge whirl-pool churned up the waves.

Balor looked down at the three babies in the basket and a tear dripped from his small left eye. It ran down his cheek and dropped into the basket. No tears came from his right eye. He began to speak. His voice sounded like rocks crushing sea-shells.

"Long ago a witch came to my door," he said to the babies. "She looked into my future. She said my daughter would have a son who would try and kill me. So I locked my daughter in a tower, where no man could reach her. I thought I was safe."

Balor stared down at the sea, at the whirl-pool.

"But a man did find her," he went on. "And I will find him. I will find the man who is the father of my daughter's children and I will kill him. I will rip him apart for making me do this."

Then Balor threw the basket out over the sea. The three babies shrieked as they fell. They hit the water and vanished under the waves. Balor turned away and walked back towards his fortress. Down in the water, one baby swam back up. On the shore, in the shadows at the bottom of the cliff, another woman stood waiting. Her hair was long and black and the wind blew it across her face. As soon as Balor turned away, she threw off her green cloak and dived into the freezing cold water.

The babies were half Fomorian and the Fomorians were good swimmers. They did not drown easily. But the whirl-pool dragged the first two away. Their weak bodies were

sucked down to the bottom of the sea. They became food for the things that lived down there.

The woman grabbed the third little boy just as the current started to pull him towards the whirl-pool. She swam back to the shore with strong strokes. She climbed up onto the rocks and wrapped her green cloak around herself and the child to keep them both warm.

"You are strong, little one," she said to the boy. "I think you'll live. And that monster, Balor – your grandfather – that piece of scum, will never know that one of his grandsons is alive."

Chapter 2
MacLeer's Son

MacLeer liked women. Everyone said it. But when he heard a knock on his door one night and opened it to see a beautiful woman standing outside, even he was suprised. Women did not often come to his door. Normally, he had to chase them. He liked it better that way. And he did not like the look of the rolled up blanket the woman had in her arms.

"Are you MacLeer, the smith?" the woman asked.

Her face was in shadow under the hood of her dark green cloak but MacLeer could see her pale skin, her full red lips and her black hair. There was a dangerous look in her eyes.

"Who's asking?" he said.

"I have many names," the woman answered. "None of them matter for now. Some people call me a fairy, others call me a witch. Ireland is my home, my island. But this belongs to you."

She put the bundle in his arms. It started to cry. MacLeer nearly dropped it in shock.

"What in the name of the goddess Danu is this?" he shouted. "What do you expect me to do with a child?"

"His name is Lug," the woman told him. "And I expect you to do what any father should do. His mother is Balor's daughter. You might remember her. You climbed into her tower about nine months ago."

"Oh, right," MacLeer said. He gave a shrug and grinned. "I didn't think anyone knew about that. I remember her now. A very lonely girl. Lovely fins."

"Take care, MacLeer," the woman said. "Balor will kill you and the child if he finds out who you are. And it will not be an easy death."

Then she was gone, vanishing into the darkness. MacLeer held the child carefully. He opened up the blanket to see the baby's face.

"Well, you've got your father's good looks," he said. "What are we going to do with you, eh? This is a fine mess altogether. And it won't help my love life either. Still, I always wanted a son. Come on then, let's find you some milk."

Before he went in, MacLeer looked out over the beach that lay in front of his small house. There wasn't much to see in the darkness. He loved the ocean, and loved sailing on it. But the Fomorians ruled the water and only a fool made them angry.

Out on the horizon, far away, he saw the dots of light that marked Tory Island. A shiver ran down his back as he thought about Balor of the Evil Eye.

"Balor's daughter," he muttered to the baby. "In the name of the goddess, how stupid can a man get? I'm always leaping without looking – that's my problem. I tell you, boy, that's the last time I climb into any towers."

Chapter 3
The King's Right Arm

When he was very little Lug began to work with MacLeer. He learned his father's trade quickly. MacLeer was a smith, a craftsman. His people were called the Dey Danann. They were known across Ireland for their skills in working bronze or stone or wood. MacLeer was one of the best smiths of the Dey Danann. He could work with any material and make almost anything, but it was his boats that made him famous. That was how he got his name – MacLeer. It meant "Son of the Sea".

But MacLeer was also a master of weapons and he taught his son how to make them and how to use them. By the time Lug was ten years old, he was already an expert smith.

One day, he took a break from work to go swimming in the sea. It was a roasting hot day, and the water of the Atlantic was lovely and cold. Lug was a superb swimmer. Perhaps it was his Fomorian blood, but he could hold his breath under water for almost an hour. He was happy in the water, he loved the way it cooled his skin.

After some time, he saw it was getting late. The sun was sinking low in the sky. He swam back to the beach and sprinted home. His father was sure to be angry. But when he arrived, MacLeer was talking to one of the neighbours at the gate. Both men looked worried. MacLeer said goodbye to the other man and hurried back into his work-shop.

"Lug!" he called out. "Bring me all the bronze we have. Get more wood for the fire. We'll need iron too. We need to make swords and spears ... and we need them fast."

"What's wrong, Pa?" Lug asked.

MacLeer didn't hear. He looked at the work-shop and at the house behind it. They were wooden huts with roofs made of straw. Even the fence around them was only made to keep out animals.

"We won't be safe here," MacLeer said. "We'll have to leave as soon as we're done."

"Pa, what's wrong?" Lug asked again. He was starting to get scared.

"Nuada, our king, has been hurt in a battle," MacLeer told his son. "His right arm was cut off. A man cannot be king with only one arm. Nuada has given up his throne. His cousin Bres is now the King of the Dey Danann, the King of Ireland. May the goddess have mercy on us all!"

"What's so bad about Bres?" Lug said. "He's a good man isn't he?"

"Bres is a friend of the Fomorians, lad," MacLeer growled. "And he'll let them walk right into our land. They'll come here to raid Donegal first. But we're not going to let that happen. Some of us will stand and fight. Now get that fire going! We've work to do!"

MacLeer grabbed the tongs and picked up a piece of iron with them. It was already cast into the shape of a sword. He heated it up in the fire until it glowed red. Then he laid it on the anvil and started to hammer at it. Iron was not like bronze – it was harder to mould into a shape. MacLeer was the only man in Ireland who knew how to craft iron. Lug was only beginning to learn its secrets.

Lug stood frozen for a moment. He had never seen fear on his father's face before. It shook him to his bones.

But standing round would do no good. He ran round the back to the wood pile to get logs for the fire. Lug could craft bronze, but they did not have much ready. He needed to smelt all the copper and tin they had, and mix it the right way to make the bronze. Only then could he start making weapons.

Chapter 4
The Fomorians

MacLeer was pounding metal on the anvil, so he and his son did not hear the chariots coming. They were almost at the gate when the boy saw them. He dropped the wood he was carrying and ran into the work-shop. MacLeer looked up and then he saw the chariots too. It was Balor with a gang of Fomorians behind him. MacLeer tried not to let the terror show on his face, but Lug saw it anyway.

"Run, Lug!" his father said. "He doesn't know you are his grandson, and he must never know. Run for your life and don't look back."

"I'm not leaving, Pa. We can fight them together," Lug snapped at him.

"It's no good fighting Balor," MacLeer told him. "Do as I say. Go now. I'll be fine. I'm sure they just want me to build some boats. Or weapons. Or ... or ... I don't know, sea-shell ear-rings or something. Who knows? We can fight them another day. But they must not see you."

"Pa! I'm not going!"

"Obey me, boy!" MacLeer shouted. "Do as I tell you or you'll get my foot up your backside! Go now!"

Lug was more afraid of his father's temper than he was of the Fomorians. He picked up a sword, a spear and his cloak and ran round the back of the work-shop. There was a forest on the hill behind MacLeer's land. Lug stopped when he reached the trees. He hid behind the trunk of an oak tree and watched.

Balor and his warriors came up to MacLeer's gate. Clouds of dust followed them, settling around them when they stopped. The Fomorian chariots were pulled by the weirdest animals Lug had ever seen. They looked like sharks and other sea creatures, but they had legs instead of fins.

Balor stepped down from his chariot and kicked the gate open. Lug gasped at the sight of the Fomorian king. This was the monster his father had told him about – the grandfather who'd tried to kill him. Balor was a giant, and with his strange helmet and armour, he looked terrifying. MacLeer came out to greet him with a smile.

"Lord Balor! What can I do for you today? Do you need some fish-hooks perhaps? Or maybe a collar for each of your men?"

"Are you MacLeer, the smith?" Balor hissed.

"That I am," MacLeer replied.

"I hear you've a great taste for women," Balor said. "Have you ever been to Tory Island? We have many fine beauties there."

"When I was young, perhaps," MacLeer answered. He was looking very nervous now. "But I'm a bit of a home-bird now. Don't like to go out much."

With a snarl, Balor reached out and grabbed him by the neck. Lifting the smith off his feet, he shoved MacLeer back into the work-shop. Lug moved to another tree and another, trying to see. But the work-shop door could not be seen from the hillside.

There came the sound of hammering. Lug heard his father scream.

"No!" Lug shouted.

He ran down the hillside. His father shrieked again. The Fomorians were laughing. Lug was only ten years old. The sword in his hand was almost taller than him, but he lifted it up over his head. Suddenly, there was a flash of light from the work-shop. The back wall exploded outwards. The blast blew Lug off his feet. He hit the ground and blacked out.

When he woke, Balor was standing over him. The sea demon stared down at him. Balor put his foot on Lug's chest so that the boy could not breathe.

"You must be MacLeer's son," the Fomorian grunted. "You may come looking for revenge one day, boy. When you become a man. Many have tried to kill me and they are

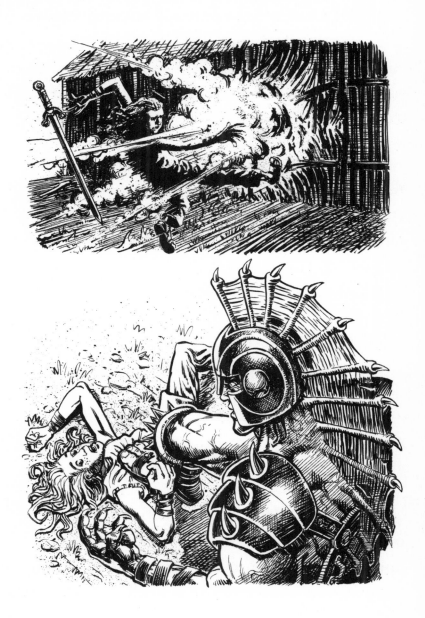

all dead. Learn from that. Go to your father, boy. I had to kill my grandchildren because of him. Take a good look at him now. See what happens to anyone who angers Balor of the Evil Eye."

Balor lifted his foot off Lug's chest and bent down closer, his face right over Lug's. He touched the ugly, wrinkled eyelids of his right eye. For a moment Lug had a strange feeling. It seemed to him that even Balor was scared of his terrible eye.

"And I hardly opened it," the Fomorian said softly. "I hardly opened it at all."

As Balor walked back to his chariot, Lug stood up slowly and limped into the workshop.

MacLeer's dead body was bent backwards over the anvil. There were bronze spear heads stuck through his hands, hammered into the workbench. But this was not why Lug screamed. It was the smell of burnt meat that made him cry. It was the sight of his father with all the flesh blasted from his head, neck and chest. There was nothing left of MacLeer's upper body but burnt bones.

This was what happened when Balor opened his eye.

Chapter 5
A Council at Tara

Seven years passed and King Bres let the Fomorians run wild across Ireland. The Dey Danann were forced to work night and day for the sea demons. Their children were taken as slaves. Every year, the people were taxed two-thirds of their crops and cattle. They began to starve.

In the seventh year something had changed. The Dey Denann began to hear news of their old king. Nuada's right arm had been made new again. The people were afraid to believe it. Then, one cold winter's day, messengers were sent to all the tribes. All the chieftains of Ireland were called to Tara for a council with the new king. Bres was gone. Nuada was King once more.

Lug was now seventeen, and keen for a chance to fight the Fomorians. He left the wild lands of Donegal and made his way to Tara. When he got there, the gates were closed. The council had already begun. A chill wind blew across the hillside. Snow was starting to fall. The countryside and forest around him were already turning white. He wrapped his cloak tightly about him.

Guards kept watch behind the fence that ran along the top of the wall. A powerful-looking warrior stood by the gate. Lug was a man now, tall and strong. His hands were rough from work, his mind was sharp from training in combat and the arts. Ever since his father's death he had spent every day getting ready for this moment. He walked up to the gate and put his pack and weapons on the ground. He shouted up to the guard.

"I am Lug, son of MacLeer!" he called. "I want to speak to my king."

"Do you indeed?" the warrior replied. "My name is Ogma, and I say you'll see him soon enough. When he leads us all into battle against the Fomorians. We will face Balor's army out west on the Plain of Weeping. You'll be welcome to join us then. Until then, King Nuada is busy meeting the chieftains and the masters of skills. Are you a master of anything, young Lug?"

Lug stared back at the other man, who was smiling at him. The guard rested his hands on his spear and looked down at the younger man. Ogma was huge, with wide shoulders and thick arms. His red beard was

thick and his skin was like leather. He looked tough and cunning.

"I am a master of many skills," Lug called back. "I am a carpenter and a metal worker, like my father before me."

"We already have the best craftsmen in the land," Ogma replied.

"I am a sailor, a fisherman and a map-maker," Lug told him.

"We're drowning in all three," Ogma called back. "Try again!"

"I am a master of chess, of music and poetry," Lug said.

"And you're modest too, by the goddess!" Ogma shouted. The other guards laughed. He looked down at Lug. "We have enough chess players and music-makers. And this is

Ireland. We have poetry coming out of our backsides. Try again."

Lug gritted his teeth. The man was starting to annoy him.

"You say you have masters for each of these skills?" he shouted and he held up his spear. "Do you have *one man* who has mastered them *all*? Let me try one more time. I am a *warrior*! I will fight your champion for the right to meet my king! Send him out to me and I'll make him cry like a baby taken from his mother's breast!"

"You want to face our champion, eh?" Ogma snorted.

The warrior put his spear to one side. With one bound, he jumped right over the fence which ran along the top of the wall. He landed on the ground in front of Lug.

"Our champion?" he said, showing his teeth. "That would be me. And I can promise you boy, I'll not be the one crying for his mother."

They agreed to fight with sticks. Two wooden staffs were thrown down by a man on the wall. Lug and Ogma faced each other, their weapons at the ready. Ogma nodded and the fight began. The sticks moved at lightning speed. Each hit was blocked and thrown back. Wood cracked against wood. Ogma was a great fighter, made hard by years of battle. Lug was young, quick and well-trained. And he was driven by a mad need to get through that gate. He had to talk to Nuada.

The two warriors danced around each other. They struck out, deflected and blocked in a blur of movement. Ogma jabbed with the end of his stick and just missed Lug's groin. Lug knocked the blow aside and smacked his staff into Ogma's knee-cap.

Ogma grunted, but it didn't slow him down. He swung his stick at Lug's head.

Lug jerked back, but not quite fast enough. The stick cut his cheek, nearly hitting his nose. Lug whipped his stick down hard, smacking Ogma's fingers. The older man flinched and pulled his hand back.

Lug saw his chance. He swept Ogma's stick to one side and jabbed the older man in the chest. The hit knocked the air out of Ogma's lungs. And as he tried to raise his stick, Lug hooked the feet out from under him. Ogma landed flat on his back on the frozen ground. Lug swung his stick down and stopped it just before it crushed Ogma's throat. The fight was over.

"A good scrap," Ogma said, panting. "You're more than a master of boasting after all. But tell me lad, why are you so keen to see Nuada? Do you really want to go up against the Fomorians? Don't you know what Balor can do?"

"I know exactly what he can do," Lug growled. He reached down and helped the other man up. "That's why I have to see Nuada. I'm going to show him the weapon that can kill Balor of the Evil Eye."

"Something that can destroy the Evil Eye?" Ogma grunted. "I'll believe it when I see it."

Chapter 6
The Road to Battle

The Dey Danann forces marched through the blizzard towards Moy Tura, the Plain of Weeping. The wind bit into their skin. The snow lay heavy on the shoulders of their cloaks. Lug rode on horseback beside the king's chariot. Every now and then, he thought he saw a woman in a green cloak riding along on a horse, far off to their right. She was partly hidden by the snow and it was hard for Lug to keep his eyes on her. He thought about the rumours he had heard. Rumours of witches who worked for the king.

Lug stared at King Nuada's right arm again. He could hardly keep his eyes off it. The king's arm had been chopped off just below the elbow seven years ago. Now it was made new again. But the lower arm was crafted from solid silver.

Nuada stood beside his chariot driver. The king was a lean man with a kind face and intelligent eyes. He had the grace of a dancer. All Ireland knew how brave he was. When he saw Lug staring at his arm, he laughed. He flexed the silver hand, opening and closing the metal fingers.

"It's beautiful, isn't it?" the king said. He held his arm up so that Lug could have a better look. "The best healers and craftsmen worked for years to make it. I wouldn't take back my place as king until I could play the harp with this hand. But I'm still not as good as the Dagda here!"

The Dagda was the king's chief bard – a singer and story-teller. He laughed at Nuada. "You are too modest, my king," he said.

The Dagda rode on the other side of the king's chariot. Lug did not like him. The Dagda was tall and thin with black hair and beard. He could sing wonderful songs and played their music on his harp. But he acted as if he was better than everyone else and only talked to the king and no one else. There were rumours too that he used dark magic.

The Dagda was an important warrior which was unusual. Music-makers did not fight battles.

Nuada tucked his silver arm under his cloak again. The metal was cold against his skin.

The king looked over at Lug. "I hope this ... this 'sling-shot' weapon of yours can do what you say. If it doesn't work, Balor's eye will kill us all."

"How did he get the evil eye?" Lug asked. "I mean, it doesn't ... it doesn't even seem to fit in his head properly."

It was the Dagda who answered.

"When Balor was a child, he went to spy on some magicians who were using dark magic. He watched through a hole in the wall of their hut. The magicians wore blind-folds as they cast their spell, but the unholy light entered Balor's eye and changed it. And, as he grew, so did the eye's power. Now he can hardly control it. He needs a special helmet to open the eye and it takes four men to hold him steady when he uses its power. To kill Balor, we must destroy the eye."

The blizzard started to lift. The snow thinned out, but the wind still chilled their bones. They were passing a small lake, the surface of the water was frozen over. They heard the beat of drums. From up ahead, they heard a Dey Danann scout blow his horn.

"We have reached the field of battle," Nuada said. "And so have the Formorians."

Chapter 7
The Screams of the Dying

As the falling snow began to clear, Lug
took his place beside Nuada, the Dagda and
Ogma. They were standing on Moy Tura, the
Plain of Weeping. Across the plain, they saw
a long line of snarling faces. The Fomorians.
There were thousands of them. They were
chanting harsh battle-cries. Lug felt a wave
of cold go through him that had nothing to do
with the weather.

"Lug," said Nuada.

"Yes, my king?" Lug replied.

"This might be a good time to put your weapon together."

"Ah, yes."

Lug jumped off his horse and untied his pack. Quickly he started to fit the weapon together. Nuada rode up and down the front line of his army, shouting at the top of his voice.

"They made slaves of our people!" he bellowed. "They beat us and tortured us and stole the food from our mouths! They took our women and children! But it all ends today! Show these demons what it means to fight the Dey Danann! Send them to their deaths!"

He lifted his spear over his head.

"Feed the earth with their blood!"

The king's army let out a massive roar. The warriors of the Dey Danann rushed forward, keen to clash with their enemy. Lug cursed and picked up the pieces of his weapon, trying to keep up with the army. He put them together as he ran. The thunder of two armies charging shook the ground beneath his feet.

The weapon worked like a sling-shot, but was much more powerful.

Lug pulled the cords back as he ran. He bent the arms back and slotted an arrow into place. The Fomorians were storming forward, bellowing their heads off, thirsty for blood. Lug stopped long enough to take aim. He fired the iron-tipped arrow.

The arrow flew a hundred metres. It punched through the helmet of one Formorian, burst out on the other side and slammed into the chest of another. They both dropped dead.

"Go on ya boy ya!" Nuada shouted over to him. Then, to the rest of his men, he yelled – "Where's Balor? Does anyone see Balor?"

But no one could see the sea demons' king. The two armies crashed into each other like the meeting of two oceans. The sling-shot was no good in close combat. Lug threw it and the bundle of arrows into the king's chariot. He had left his spear and shield behind, but he still had his sword.

Moments later, he was fighting for his life. All around him, weapons clashed, blades cut and clubs crushed. Shields were dented and smashed. Blood spurted from wounds and the screaming of the wounded and dying began. Lug dashed through the madness, thrusting and jabbing his blade into Fomorian flesh.

Ogma was tackling three of the sea demons.

"Where's Balor?" Ogma yelled as he cut the third one down. "I see Indeck, their champion, but where is their chieftain?"

He left Lug and pushed his way through to Indeck, keen to show the Fomorian warrior his blade. Lug waited for a moment. The fighting went on all around him. On a hill above the battle, he saw the woman in the green cloak. Her long black hair whipped around her in the wind. Who was she? She pointed back the way he had come. He looked back.

He could see over most of the battlefield. He stared back at the lake they had passed before the battle. Something burst up from the ice. Fomorians rose up from the freezing water. They had been waiting under the ice all this time. They followed Balor of the Evil Eye. The sea demons rushed out onto the hill and four of them tied ropes to Balor's armour.

"They're behind us!" Lug shouted. "Balor is behind us!"

But no one heard him over the noise of the fighting. A horn sounded and suddenly all the Fomorians broke away from the battle and ran back. The Dey Danann watched. They couldn't understand what was happening. Then they heard Lug and saw him pointing.

Balor's men were standing behind their king, all except for the four who were holding him in place with the ropes. Balor put his hand up to his helmet. The helmet had a lever that opened the lids of his evil eye. Panic spread across the Dey Danann forces. They turned to run, but it was too late. They were trapped.

Balor opened his eye.

Chapter 8
The Battle is Lost

It was like looking right into the sun. Lug dived behind a heap of dead bodies before the beam of Balor's eye could burn him alive. All across the plain, men screamed as their flesh was blasted from their bones. Balor could hardly control the eye's power. Veins stood out on his face and neck. In one pass, the eye killed nearly a hundred warriors.

The eye missed Nuada on its first pass. He picked up Lug's sling-shot and charged his

chariot straight for the Fomorian leader. He roared his battle-cry as he fired an arrow.

The arrow thudded into Balor's arm. The sea demon snarled in pain as he pulled the arrow out. Then he turned his eye on Nuada. The king's body burst into flame. The force of the blast ripped burning flesh from his skeleton. His horses exploded in front of him and Nuada's shriek was cut short as he died. Lug looked on in horror.

The battle was over. The Dey Danann had lost.

As the beam from Balor's eye swept back and forth over the battlefield, Lug lay still, flat on the ground. Then slowly he crawled towards the body of his king. Apart from Nuada's legs, all that was left of him was a scorched skeleton and the silver arm.

The chariot was still on fire, and so were the dead bodies of the horses. Lug grabbed the sling-shot before its wooden parts caught fire too. He swore when he saw the arrows. They were already burnt, only the iron tips were left. The sling-shot was useless without arrows.

But there was one thing he could use. He stretched forward into the flames and hoped his king would forgive him ...

Moments later, Lug was crawling on his belly across the snow. He tried to stay hidden among the dead bodies. Balor was still sweeping the plain with his eye. More than once, Lug felt the heat of it across his back. He had to get close to the Fomorian. He would only get one chance. And he would have to look Balor right in the eye when he took his shot.

Lug reached the edge of the lake. The ice was broken and he crawled in. He gasped in shock at the coldness of the water as he slid under the surface. And then he waited.

Sometimes the beam passed over his head and he felt it heat the water around him. But mostly there was just the freezing cold. Ice started to form on the surface. Lug curled into a ball to try and keep his hands and feet from going numb. Lug could go for a long time without air, but the cold was seeping deep into his body. When the time came to move, he would have to move fast. But he was losing the feeling in his arms and legs.

Up on the hill, Lug saw the four men let go of the ropes that held Balor steady. They stood up, groaned and rubbed their scorched skin. Their leader's eye was closed again. Lug flexed his arms and legs slowly. He jammed his feet into the ground, ready to push himself out of the water. The Fomorians were crossing the plain. They were cheering and waving their fists and weapons. Lug blew out through his teeth. The bubbles rose through the freezing water.

And then he burst up through the surface. As he took aim with the sling-shot, he roared at Balor.

"Hey, Grandpa! Feast your eye on this!"

And then he fired. There were no arrows left, so Lug used the only thing he had. Nuada's silver arm. It all happened in an instant. The arm shot through the air, the fingers opening as they flew. Balor was already reaching for his helmet. The eye began to open. Lug thought he saw a look of relief on Balor's face just before Nuada's hand punched through his head and burst out the other side.

When it hit the ground, the hand had the huge eye held tight in its fingers. The eye exploded, scattering and burning the Fomorian warriors.

Chapter 9
Stain the Snow Red

There were still many Dey Danann warriors able to fight. When they saw the explosion, they cheered and charged towards the sea demon army. They were led by Ogma and the Dagda, who struck down enemies right and left as they ran.

"Tear them open, Dey Danann!" Ogma bellowed. "Stain the snow red!"

The Fomorians turned and ran. As they fled, Lug saw a woman with wild black hair running beside them. She snarled at them and leapt into the air, whirling her green cloak. Her body seemed to break apart and turn into a giant flock of crows. The crows attacked the sea demons. They pecked at their eyes and clawed at their faces.

The Fomorians' screams faded into the distance.

The Dey Danann began to tend to their wounded. So many had died. The crying started. Songs were sung for the dead. Lug stood over the body of the Formorian king. Balor of the Evil Eye – his grandfather. Ogma came up beside him. The Dey Danann champion looked at the sling-shot and grinned.

"I always knew you'd take someone's eye out with that thing," he said.

"Nuada had a hand in it too," Lug told him.

"He always had a way of reaching out to people," Ogma replied sadly. "But now our king is dead. And he left no sons to take his place."

The Dagda strode up to them and dropped his heavy club on the ground. He looked worn out. Lug knew how he felt. The bard grabbed Lug's hand.

"You invented the weapon that killed our enemy. You showed loyalty, cunning and you had the nerve to take action when no one else could. But above all, I think you have a good heart, Lug of the Long Arm. If you can be noble in life as you have been in battle, I think you would make an excellent king."

"I'm sure of it," Ogma laughed. He held up Nuada's melted silver arm. "And if you don't do a good job, the old king will still be on hand to give you a slap if you need it!"

Lug gave his friend a sad smile. He turned and stared out across the Plain of Weeping. Fresh snow was starting to fall. It was covering up the blood that had been spilled. Lug was shivering now. He didn't know if that was because of the wind on his wet skin, or from the shock of battle. The Dagda handed him a cloak and Lug wrapped it around himself.

"Let's send the dead on their last journey," he said. "Then we will give our thanks to the goddess Danu. And after that, we'll go home. There will be songs sung about this battle. Stories will be told around the fire. They will make heroes of us."

He looked down at Balor's body.

"And they will make a monster of him. I pity him now. I think I always did, even when he killed my father. The real monster was in Balor's head. I think he was glad to be free of it in the end."

Lug looked up at the Dey Danann as they came towards him. There seemed to be a glow in his eyes as he spoke to them.

"The Evil Eye is destroyed. Let us bury our dead and go home to our people."

And so they did. From a far-away hill-top, the woman in the green cloak watched them leave.

Lug was crowned king of the Dey Danann at the Hill of Tara and he ruled for a long, long time. Thousands of years later, his story is still told in Ireland. Lug of the Long Arm, the only man to look straight into the Evil Eye and survive.

The Legend

This is not my story. The legend of Lug and Balor is one of thousands of tales passed down over the years by Irish story-tellers, or *seanachaí*. Before there were films or television or even books, the *seanachaí* sat by the fire and thrilled adults and children with tales of adventure, comedy and love.

Balor of the Evil Eye is one of the oldest Irish legends. It may even have been around before the Celts came to Ireland. There are stories like it in many other countries. Stories about a man or woman who could kill you, or turn you to stone, just by looking at you.

I made some of the names in this story simpler for those who don't speak any Irish. The *Tuatha Dé Danann* became the Dey Danann and *Manannán Mac Lír* became MacLeer. *Magh Tuiredh* became Moy Tura and *Indech* became Indeck. Lug should be spelled *Lugh*.

My name, Oisín, is Irish too – you say it – "Uh-Sheen", but you'd never guess that by looking at it.

The Celts spread across Europe. They came to Ireland in about 300 B.C. This really annoyed the Romans, who wanted to rule the world and make everyone speak Latin. The Celts were brave and cunning fighters. They often stripped off and fought totally naked to freak out their enemies. Sometimes their women charged into battle beside them.

The Romans thought the Celts were too loud, too rude and too fond of arguing. They loved to boast and tell wild stories about how brave they were. They told tales of great gory battles, tales of magical stones and horrible beasts and places where people just vanished.

But the Celts were not savages. They were skilled in using wood, metal, stone and cloth. They were farmers and lived in harmony with nature. They brought the Iron Age to Ireland.

They conquered Ireland, but the Romans never did. Perhaps the Romans decided not to come here after fighting the Celts in Scotland. Or maybe it was the weather that put them off … we'll never know.

The Celts left us lots of fantastic things – their weapons, metal work, carvings, and their creepy, leathery bog bodies. But the most exciting things they left us were their stories.

I hope you found *The Evil Eye* as exciting as I did when I first heard it.

Oisin McGann

Author

Favourite hero:
Charley from Charley's War. He was a normal bloke trying to do his best in a terrible war. And I loved the comic.

Favourite monster:
The shark in the first Jaws movie.

Your weapon of choice:
Medusa's eyes – they could turn people to stone.

Special secret power:
Mess with me and I'll make you into someone really nasty in one of my books.

Favourite fight scene:
There's a comic called Slaine – The Horned God. It tells the story of the battle that's in this book, and it's brilliant!

Goodie or baddie:
A goodie who isn't always good, or a baddie who feels bad about what he does.

RELOADED

Balor

Bad guy

Favourite hero:
I've killed hundreds of heroes in my time, and I did not like any of them.

Favourite monster:
My home, the sea, is full of monsters. My favourites are the sirens — beautiful but deadly.

Your weapon of choice:
The Gae Bolga — the magical spear that could target its victims like a heat-seeking missile and never failed to kill.

Special secret power:
Read this story and find out.

Favourite fight scene:
The death of Achilles in the Trojan War.

RELOADED

Barrington Stoke would like to thank all its readers for commenting on the manuscript before publication and in particular:

Daniel Baird

Josh Clark

Ryan Connolly

Annie Dawson

Louise Denovan

Liz Devine

Kirsten Haldare

Lisa Horsburgh

Taiba Jabbar

Ryan Kelly

Ryan Ledwidge

Dean MacKay

Brogan MacKenzie

Matthew McIntyre

Ola Moleda

Lucy Morrill

Jymek Niciak

Conor Nicoll

Michael Nicol

Stacey Powell

Cherie Robertson

Daniel Rutherford

Alicia Smith

Martin Smith

Macaulay Stirling

Jodie Sweeny

Becki Symon

Rosie Whyte

Become a Consultant!

Would you like to give us feedback on our titles before they are published? Contact us at the email address below – we'd love to hear from you!

info@barringtonstoke.co.uk
www.barringtonstoke.co.uk

THE GOBLIN OF TARA

BY
OISIN MCGANN

Every Halloween, the goblin creeps in from
the Otherworld.
Every Halloween, flesh burns and bodies fall.
The people of Tara need a hero.
Step up Finn MacCool.
He's the only hope they've got ...

You can order *The Goblin of Tara* directly from
www.barringtonstoke.co.uk

WANTED: JANOSIK
BY
ANDREW MATTHEWS

Killer. Thief. Outlaw.
And he's the good guy ...
Hero to the poor. Hated by the rich.
Wanted: Janosik.
Dead Or Alive.

You can order *Wanted: Janosik* directly from
www.barringtonstoke.co.uk

THE GREAT GREEN MONSTER

BY
MAGGIE PEARSON

No one knows where it came from.
And there's no one left to ask – the monster
ate them all.
Akim and his mother are the only people left.
Could anything be worse than the great green
monster?

You can order *The Great Green Monster* directly from
www.barringtonstoke.co.uk